Dear Parent:
Your child's love of reading starts here!

Every child learns to read in a different way and at his or her own speed. Some go back and forth between reading levels and read favorite books again and again. Others read through each level in order. You can help your young reader improve and become more confident by encouraging his or her own interests and abilities. From books your child reads with you to the first books he or she reads alone, there are I Can Read Books for every stage of reading:

SHARED READING
Basic language, word repetition, and whimsical illustrations, ideal for sharing with your emergent reader

BEGINNING READING
Short sentences, familiar words, and simple concepts for children eager to read on their own

READING WITH HELP
Engaging stories, longer sentences, and language play for developing readers

READING ALONE
Complex plots, challenging vocabulary, and high-interest topics for the independent reader

ADVANCED READING
Short paragraphs, chapters, and exciting themes for the perfect bridge to chapter books

I Can Read Books have introduced children to the joy of reading since 1957. Featuring award-winning authors and illustrators and a fabulous cast of beloved characters, I Can Read Books set the standard for beginning readers.

A lifetime of discovery begins with the magical words "I Can Read!"

Visit www.icanread.com for information
on enriching your child's reading experience.

The Dark Knight: I Am Batman

BATMAN and all related characters and elements are trademarks of DC Comics © 2008.

All Rights Reserved.

Printed in the United States of America.

No part of this book may be used or reproduced in any manner whatsoever without written permission except in the case of brief quotations embodied in critical articles and reviews.

For information address HarperCollins Children's Books, a division of HarperCollins Publishers, 10 East 53rd Street, New York, NY 10022.

www.icanread.com

Library of Congress catalog number: 2008923459

ISBN 978-0-06-156189-4

Cover art by Cameron Stewart and Dave McCaig

Book design by John Sazaklis

❖

12 13 LP/WOR 20 19 18 17 16 15   First Edition

I Can Read!

READING 2 WITH HELP

THE DARK KNIGHT

I AM BATMAN

ADAPTED BY **CATHERINE HAPKA**
PENCILS BY **ADRIAN BARRIOS**
DIGITAL PAINTS BY **KANILA TRIPP**

INSPIRED BY THE FILM **THE DARK KNIGHT**
SCREENPLAY BY
JONATHAN NOLAN AND **CHRISTOPHER NOLAN**
STORY BY **CHRISTOPHER NOLAN & DAVID S. GOYER**
BATMAN CREATED BY **BOB KANE**

HarperCollins*Publishers*

I have nice clothes.

I have a fast car.

And I have lots of other fancy toys and gadgets.

Most people think my life is easy.

But they don't know my secret.

By night I become Batman,

the defender of Gotham City.

There's the Bat-Signal!
That means it is time
for me to go to work.

I need a lot of high-tech stuff
to help me keep Gotham safe.

My friend Lucius Fox helps me.

He works for my company.

But his most important job

is inventing all of Batman's tools.

I rush to my secret Bat-Bunker.

It lies deep underground.

The only way to get in

is by a hidden elevator.

The Bat-Bunker hides

the crime-fighting gear

that Lucius invents for me.

13

I put on my Batsuit.

A mask hides my face

so no one will know who I am.

The suit has strong armor

to protect me in a fight.

It also has a cape and a tool belt.

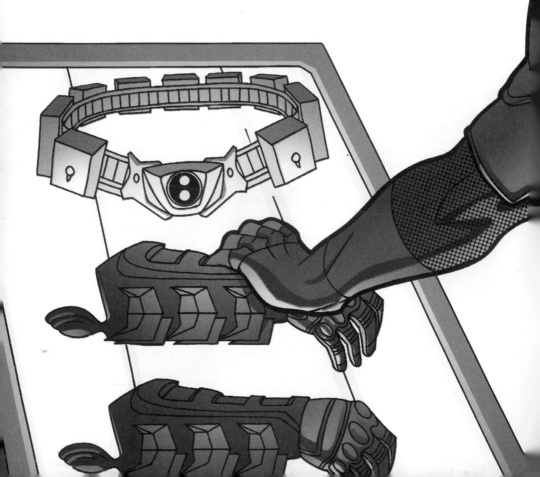

Sometimes I drive the Batmobile.

It has strong armor

and can make long jumps.

The Batmobile also has tires
that can ride over anything.

But today I ride the Bat-Pod.

It is very fast.

It has strong armor, too.

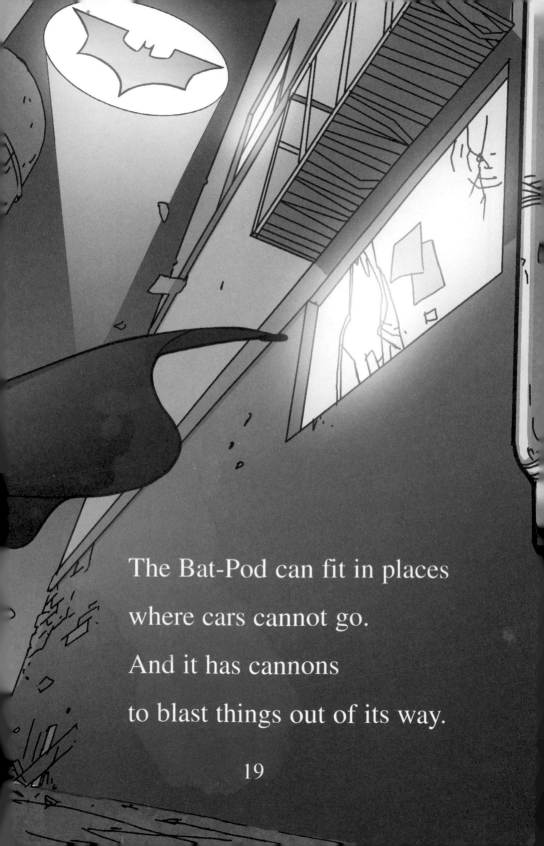

The Bat-Pod can fit in places
where cars cannot go.
And it has cannons
to blast things out of its way.

Police Lieutenant Gordon

calls me to a bank.

Someone just robbed it!

I use a gadget to scan the cash.

It gives me clues.

The robber is the Joker!

Now I can track him down.

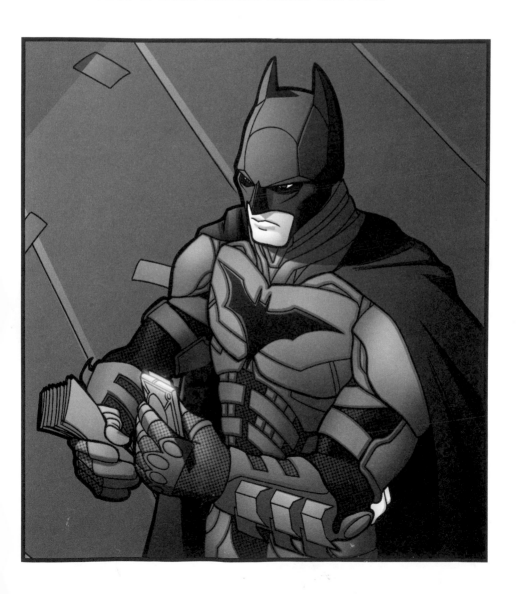

The Joker is a tricky foe.

His jokes are never funny.

Sometimes they hurt people.

I will need all of my tools

to find the Joker

and make him pay for his crime.

That night, my friend Rachel
throws me a surprise birthday party.

A clown appears
and makes the guests laugh.
"Wait a minute," Rachel says.
"I didn't hire a clown."
Uh-oh! That's no clown.
That's the Joker!

The Joker tosses a smoke bomb.

Knockout gas comes out of it.

All the party guests start to yawn.

They fall fast asleep.

The Joker begins to rob them!

Quickly, I put on my Batsuit
and my gas mask.
The mask keeps me from
breathing the knockout gas.

Now is my chance to catch the Joker.

He won't get away this time!

I throw my Batarang

at the fire sprinklers.

The sprinklers turn on.

The water makes the gas go away.

Everyone is soaked!

The Joker tries to escape.

But I catch him and tie him up.

Now the joke is on him.

He'll spend a long time in jail!

Fighting crime is not easy.

But my gear and gadgets

help make it all possible.

I am not just Bruce Wayne.

I am Batman!